Teddy Long Legs

One sunny morning, Tiffo and Teddy were playing chase-the-stick. Teddy threw the stick so high, it got caught in the branches of the tree.

Teddy said they could find another stick to play with, but Tiffo told Teddy that this was his favourite stick.

Teddy and Tiffo jumped as high as they could, but the stick was out of reach.

Then Missy Hissy offered to slither up the tree and get the stick. But the tree trunk was too slippery for her to climb.

Tiffo's favourite stick was gone.

Andy Pandy had just finished painting Looby Loo's door when Teddy walked past.
Andy Pandy thought Teddy looked sad.

Teddy told Andy Pandy about losing Tiffo's favourite stick in the tree.

Andy Pandy said that if Teddy came to his house, he'd try to help.

He told Teddy to bring the empty paint pots from Looby Loo's house with him.

Andy Pandy got some paints and paintbrushes, some stickers and some rope.

He told Teddy to paint the outsides of the pots.

Andy Pandy said they were ready.
"Ready for what?" wondered Teddy.

Andy Pandy explained that they'd made a pair of stilts. The stilts would make Teddy's legs longer, so he'd be tall enough to reach the stick.

The stilts made Teddy just tall enough to reach Tiffo's stick. At last he had rescued it!

But Tiffo had forgotten all about his favourite stick. He had found a new stick to play with. Tiffo tossed his new stick into the air...

...and chased it into the garden, where it landed at Teddy's feet.

Teddy told Tiffo how he had got Tiffo's favourite stick out of the tree using a pair of stilts.

But Andy Pandy said that Teddy still had a
new toy.

"Hooray!" shouted Teddy, walking away on his
new stilts.